D0331390

CASEBUSTERS

Beware the Pirate Ghost

Adventures in the CASEBUSTERS series:

The Statue Walks at Night

The Legend of Deadman's Mine

Backstage with a Ghost

Check in to Danger

The House Has Eyes

Secret of the Time Capsule

Beware the Pirate Ghost

Disney
Adventures
(7)

CASEBUSTERS

Beware the Pirate Ghost

By Joan Lowery Nixon

Disney
PRESS

New York

For Bridget Elizabeth Quinlan with my love
—J. L. N.

Text © 1996 by Joan Lowery Nixon.

Printed in the United States of America.
First Edition
1 3 5 7 9 10 8 6 4 2

Library of Congress Catalog Card Number: 95-83884
ISBN: 0-7868-3102-2 (trade)/0-7868-4080-3 (pbk.)

1

BRIAN AND SEAN WOKE to a loud pounding on their front door. "Go away! It's Saturday!" Sean grumbled and stuck his head under the blanket.

But as soon as he heard Brian, Mom, and Dad racing down the stairs, he tumbled out of bed, pulled on his jeans, and ran downstairs, too. Following the sound of voices, he burst into the living room.

A man and a woman were both talking at the same time. The man's face was red and blotchy, and he waved his arms excitedly. The woman wiped away tears and blew her nose.

Nobody stopped to introduce Sean, but it didn't matter. He recognized Mr. and Mrs. Kingsley Hopper—parents of the most spoiled seven-year-old brat he and Brian had ever met.

"Lester's bed had been slept in, and there was no sign of a struggle," Mr. Hopper shouted.

"You've got to help us! You're a private investigator. You've got to find our son!" Mrs. Hopper screeched.

John Quinn raised his voice. "Quiet, *please*," he said firmly.

Both Hoppers stopped talking and stared at him.

"Please sit down," Mrs. Quinn said. She led the Hoppers to comfortable chairs and patted Mrs. Hopper's shoulder in sympathy.

When everyone was seated, Mr. Quinn

said, "Let's start at the beginning. When you discovered your son was missing, did you call the police?"

"Oh, no! We couldn't!" Mr. Hopper said. "The kidnappers warned us not to."

Sean poked Brian. "Who'd want Lester?" he whispered.

Mrs. Hopper pulled a folded paper from her handbag. Her fingers trembled as she held it out to Mr. Quinn. "This is the ransom note left by Lester's kidnappers," she said.

Brian and Sean jumped up and leaned over their dad's shoulders to read the note:

YOUR SUN HAS BEEN KIDNAPED. DO NOT GO TO THE POLICE OR YOU'LL NEVER SEE LESTER AGIN. GET A LOT OF MUNEY READY. YOU'LL HERE FROM US SOON.

The ransom note was crudely printed, and some of the words were misspelled.

"Any chance Lester wrote this himself?" Sean asked.

Mrs. Hopper gasped. "How can you possibly think that Lester wrote his own ransom note? That's absurd! Besides, Lester is a very bright boy, way ahead of everyone in his class. He always makes A-plus in spelling."

"Uh, Mrs. Hopper," Brian suggested, "Lester might have tried to make the note look like someone else wrote it."

"Nonsense. What reason would Lester have for pretending to be kidnapped?" Mr. Hopper asked.

Brian shrugged. "Lester might have wanted to throw you off the track while he ran away," he said. "Didn't he run away from home last year?"

Mrs. Hopper gasped. "I don't care what you

heard or read about in the newspaper. Lester did not run away. He simply wanted to visit his grandmother."

"In the middle of the night?" Sean asked.

Mr. Hopper turned so red he looked as if he might explode. "I can't believe what I'm hearing! Lester is a perfectly well-behaved child."

"That's enough, boys. Sit down," Mr. Quinn warned.

Brian and Sean knew they'd better keep their opinions to themselves, at least for now, so they went back to their chairs.

Mrs. Hopper burst into tears again. "We didn't tell you about a problem that makes everything much, much worse," she said. "The cold we thought Lester had . . . yesterday his doctor found it was a lung infection. He prescribed medication that must be taken regularly or there could be complications."

"That's right," Mr. Hopper said. "Lester had his first dose at nine yesterday morning, and his second at nine last night. He should have another dose within twelve hours—by nine o'clock this morning."

Everyone turned to look at the clock on the mantel.

"Oh, dear," Mrs. Quinn murmured. "It's almost six-thirty."

Mr. Hopper nodded. "Lester's doctor said the dose could be delayed a short while, but absolutely no longer than eighteen hours. That means if Lester isn't found before three o'clock this afternoon, his life will be in danger!"

"Does Lester know this?" Mrs. Quinn asked.

"No," Mr. Hopper admitted. "Lester gets upset easily, and we didn't want to frighten him."

He looked pleadingly at John Quinn. "We're desperate, John. Please take the case," he said. "We're counting on you to find Lester."

2

MRS. QUINN LEFT TO GET dressed, and Mr. Quinn opened his notebook. Brian and Sean sat very quietly, hoping that no one would notice they were in the room. They wanted to hear the questions their dad would ask the Hoppers, and they especially wanted to hear the answers.

"Let's go over your activities last night," Mr. Quinn said to Mr. and Mrs. Hopper. "Were there any problems?"

"Oh, no," Mrs. Hopper said quickly.

"None at all," Mr. Hopper added.

"You gave Lester his medicine?"

"At nine o'clock."

"Did he take it without complaint?"

Mr. Hopper hesitated. "He didn't like the taste of the medicine, but . . ."

Mrs. Hopper interrupted. "He's a very dear, obedient little boy. He took a spoonful of his medicine. Then I tucked him into bed myself. He smiled and settled down without a fuss."

Sean glanced at Brian and slowly shook his head. That didn't sound like the Lester he knew.

"Have you called Lester's grandmother?" Mr. Quinn asked.

"Yes. She's the only one we've told, besides you. But she hasn't heard from Lester," Mr. Hopper said.

Mrs. Hopper clasped her hands to her cheeks. "Why ask about his grandmother?" she cried. "I know! It's because of what happened last year. You don't believe that Lester was kidnapped, do you?"

"As a private investigator, I keep an open mind while I collect facts," Mr. Quinn answered calmly. "I'd like to see Lester's room and examine your house."

"The house . . . yes." Mr. Hopper gripped the arms of his chair. "We didn't get around to telling you that Lester's window was open, and the screen was lying on the ground. Whoever kidnapped Lester must have got in through his bedroom window."

"I'll check the windowsill and frame for fingerprints," Mr. Quinn said, "and the kidnappers' note, as well."

He stood up and said to the Hoppers, "Please give me your address and telephone number. I'll dress and meet you at your house within a half an hour."

Brian motioned to Sean, and they hurried upstairs.

"Do you think the Hoppers were telling the truth?" Sean asked.

"I don't know, but there's one way to find out," Brian answered.

Sean heard the shower turn on in his parents' bathroom. "Are we going to ask Dad if we can go with him?"

"No," Brian answered. "We aren't going to learn anything new talking to the Hoppers. I'd rather talk to the kids who live in the neighborhood. Kids pay attention to what's happening. They make the best witnesses."

Sean sniffed the air. The fragrance of French toast drifted up from the kitchen. "Bri, could we have breakfast first?" he begged.

Brian hesitated only a second. "Remember

that Lester has to take his medicine before three o'clock, or his life's in danger," he said. "It's nearly seven o'clock. We haven't got much time, so we'll have to eat fast."

3

BRIAN AND SEAN HOPPED on their bikes and got to the Hoppers' home just a few minutes behind their dad.

"You didn't tell me the Hoppers live right behind Debbie Jean Parker," Brian said.

"It's okay. She won't know we're here," Sean said.

"That's not what I meant. If anyone notices things, then blabs about them, it's Debbie Jean," Brian said. "I want to talk to her."

At that moment Debbie Jean appeared. "Hi," she said. "I saw you ride past my house."

"We're here on official Casebusters business," Sean said.

"You don't look very official," She said to Sean. "You've got syrup on your chin."

She laughed as Sean wiped his chin on the sleeve of his T-shirt, but Sean groaned. Why did Debbie Jean always have to butt in when he and Bri were on a case?

Brian pulled out his investigator's notebook and pen. He beckoned to some kids who were playing baseball in the street. "We'd like to ask some questions," he said.

"Sure. About what?" one of the boys asked.

"About Lester Hopper, starting with last night," Brian told them.

"Oh. You mean about the fight," Debbie Jean said.

"What fight?" Sean asked.

Debbie Jean preened. "I heard the whole

thing," she said. "Lester's bedroom window was wide open. It's on the back of their house, opposite mine. He had to take some medicine, and he didn't want to, so he had a real screaming fit. His parents yelled that he had to take the medicine, and he yelled that it tasted terrible and he wouldn't."

Brian, who'd been writing as fast as he could to keep up, finally looked at Debbie Jean. "Did he take it?"

"They must have gotten some of it inside him," Debbie Jean said, "because I heard him choking and sputtering and yelling that he wasn't ever going to take any more of that horrible stuff."

One of the baseball players stepped forward. "She's right about that," he said. "I live over there—next door to the Hoppers—and I hear a lot of that yelling, too."

"Lester is a real spoiled kid," another boy said.

"He's rude to everybody."

"He's a first-class dork."

"A real brat."

"Why are you asking all this stuff about Lester? Tell me," Debbie Jean insisted.

"Sorry, no comment," Sean said with a grin. He loved bugging Debbie Jean. "Our cases are confidential."

"What do you mean, your cases? And what's confidential?"

"We really can't talk about it, Debbie Jean," Brian said. "But we appreciate your help." He thanked the ballplayers, too, and they went back to their game.

Brian made notes on what the kids told him, as he walked across the Hoppers' yard and down their driveway. Sean followed. Debbie

Jean was right behind them.

"Does Lester have a bicycle?" Brian asked Debbie Jean.

"Sure," she answered. "Lester likes to make tire ruts across people's lawns after a rain. And he likes to ride as fast as he can down the sidewalk at people passing by, so they have to jump off into the street."

"What does his bike look like?"

"It's a mountain bike—green, with a chrome headlight and a matching water bottle."

Sean peered into the backyard and into the open garage. "I don't see a bike like that around here."

"Excuse us, Debbie Jean. Sean and I need to have a conference," Brian said.

Although she scowled at them, Brian led Sean into the Hoppers' backyard and around a tall clump of hibiscus. "We've got two facts," he said. "A missing bike and the information that Lester didn't want to take his medicine."

"We'd better tell Dad," Sean said. "Kidnappers don't take bicycles."

"Kidnappers?" Something fell through the bushes, landing at their feet. Debbie Jean scrambled to her feet, her eyes shining with excitement. "Is that what your case is about? Lester was kidnapped?"

"You're not supposed to know," Sean told her. "Nobody is supposed to know. The Hoppers don't even want to tell the police."

"That's okay. I won't tell," Debbie Jean said. "I'm going to help you solve the case."

"No, you're not," Sean said.

"I told you about the fight over taking the medicine, didn't I?"

"Yes, but—"

"And I told you about the bike. Right?"

"Right, but—"

"So I'm going to help you. If you won't let me come with you, I'll follow you. You're not going to leave me out."

"Yes, we are," Sean said. "We're going inside the Hoppers' house to talk to our dad, and you're going to stay right here."

"We'll call you if we need you," Brian said.

Brian and Sean walked around to the front door and rang the Hoppers' doorbell.

"Hey, look, Bri. Dad's car is gone," Sean said.

Mrs. Hopper opened the door. Her eyes were puffy and red, and she dabbed at her nose with a wad of tissues. "If you're looking for your father, he just left," she said.

"Do you know where he went?" Sean asked.

She sighed and said, "He convinced us that his close friend on the police force can be trusted to keep quiet—"

"Detective Thomas Kerry," Brian interrupted.

"Yeah. Detective Kerry will work with Dad and not blab stuff to the newspapers and TV," Sean said.

Mrs. Hopper bent down and stared at them. "And the two of you are not to talk about what happened either," she said.

She began to swing the door shut, but Brian quickly said, "Sean and I are helping Dad. Could we see Lester's room? Sometimes kids notice things about other kids that adults take for granted."

"We don't take anything about Lester for granted," Mrs. Hopper began, but Brian smiled and interrupted.

"Please?" he asked. "We want to do everything we can to help find Lester in time. This may be important."

Mrs. Hopper stared at Brian and Sean for a long moment. Then she said, "Very well. Come in."

She led them through a hallway to the back of the house. Lester's bedroom was large and sunny, and everything was neatly in place.

"Don't touch anything," Mrs. Hopper ordered. "Lester is a very neat boy and likes to keep his bedroom tidy."

Lester or his mother? Sean wondered.

The phone rang in another room. Mrs. Hopper gasped. "That may be the kidnappers! Don't touch anything!" she repeated, then ran to answer the phone.

Brian and Sean began to explore Lester's room.

Brian carefully examined the windowsill. He leaned out the open window to study the screen, which was still twisted and lying on the grass, and to see the hooks at the top of the window frame on which the screen had been hanging.

"No scratches around the eye that the screen had hooked into. No bent hooks at the top. No one from outside forced this screen off the window. It had to have been opened from inside," he told Sean.

"That means Lester took off the screen."

"Or at least somebody *inside* the house did."

"Do you think Dad noticed?" Sean asked.

"It would have been one of the first things he would have checked."

Sean thought about it. "If Lester wasn't kidnapped—if he's just pretending to be— where would he go?"

"Did you see all of Lester's posters?" Brian asked. "They're all of caves. Carlsbad Caverns in New Mexico and Mammoth Cave in

Kentucky."

Sean bent over the low bookcase. "He's got a whole bunch of books about caves, too." He stood up and looked at Brian. He could tell they were thinking the same thing.

"The only caves around here are the pirate caves, down at Hernando Cove," Sean said. He thought about what Brian's best friend, Sam Miyako, had told him about the pirate caves, and he shuddered. "Sam said that the pirate ghost who lives in the caves runs people through with his bloody sword. Then he feeds them to the sharks."

"Don't pay attention to Sam's stories," Brian told Sean. "You know they always give you nightmares."

"Sam knows five people who saw the pirate."

"Forget what Sam said. We're working on a missing-person case."

"Sam's not the only one who knows about the pirate ghost," Sean insisted. "Everybody knows the caves are haunted." He thought a moment and asked, "Lester wouldn't have ridden his bike in the middle of the night down to the pirate caves . . . would he?"

"The caves are dangerous," Brian said. "Nobody with any sense goes near the pirate caves, even in daylight."

"Who says Lester has any sense?" Sean asked. "Check the facts. Lester likes caves. The pirate caves are the only ones around. So . . ."

Brian finished the sentence. "So that means we ride our bikes out to the caves to see if he's there."

"And run into the pirate?" Sean had second thoughts. "Lester's only seven years old. Maybe he's sitting somewhere in a movie theater. Or maybe he slept on park bench, and right now he's feeding popcorn to the ducks."

Brian shook his head and smiled. "Good try, but it won't work. The movie theaters in Redoaks aren't open all night, and if Lester had slept on a park bench, the police on patrol would have found him and picked him up." He paused. "If you're too scared to search the pirate caves, you can stay home. I'll go by myself."

"Scared? Who, me? I'm not scared," Sean answered. "I was just being a good detective by going over all the things that could have happened to Lester."

He turned at the doorway to face Brian. "What'll we do about the pirate ghost?"

"The ghost is only a legend," Brian said. "We don't know if it's true or not."

Sean gulped. "But we're going to find out," he said. "Right?"

"Right," Brian said. He lowered his voice so

that if Mrs. Hopper happened to be nearby she wouldn't hear him. "We've got to find Lester before three o'clock, Sean. And we're not going to let a stupid ghost stop us!"

A S BRIAN AND SEAN pedaled toward
home, Brian said, "Let's stop and get
flashlights."

"And get in touch with Dad," Sean said.

They rode past Debbie Jean's house, and
Sean grinned. "I guess Debbie Jean finally paid
attention when I told her she couldn't help us,"
he said, "She was gone when we left the
Hoppers.'"

"You haven't been looking in the right
places," Brian said. He glanced over his shoulder. "She's on her bike, and she's been doing a

pretty good job of tailing us."

Sean groaned.

"Except for when she rode through some-body's vegetable garden," Brian added.

"What are we going to do about her?" Sean asked.

"Don't worry," Brian said. "We'll leave our bikes in the backyard, and after we pick up the stuff we need, we'll cut out the back way and lose her."

When Brian and Sean burst into the kitchen they discovered that neither their mom nor dad was home. They called their dad's office and got only his recorded message.

"Lester is a real nut about caves, so we're going to check out the pirate caves at Hernando Cove," Brian said as soon as he heard the beep. He went on to tell what he and Sean had found out about the argument and the missing bike.

Next, he tried to reach Detective Kerry, in case their father was still with him, but was told that Detective Kerry wasn't in the office.

"Leave a note for Mom," Sean said. He pointed to a slip of paper Mrs. Quinn had fastened to the refrigerator. On it she'd written that she was following the route Lester might have taken if he had gone to visit his grandmother.

Brian jotted down the message he'd given to Mr. Quinn.

Sean read over Brian shoulder. "I hope Mom doesn't know that the caves are haunted," he said.

"She knows they're dangerous," Brian said. "Remember a few years ago when she worked with a committee to get the county to put up warning signs?"

"The signs didn't keep kids away. The pirate ghost did," Sean said. "That's what Sam said, anyway."

The back door opened, and Sam Miyako stepped into the kitchen. "What did Sam say?" he asked.

"I was telling Bri what you said about the pirate ghost down at Hernando Cove," Sean explained. "He's real, isn't he?"

"Ghosts aren't real," Brian said. He pulled two flashlights out of a kitchen cabinet drawer. He tested them and handed one to Sean.

Sam put on a low, scary voice. "Be glad the pirate ghost didn't hear you. He'd get revenge. Someday they'd find your bones buried deep beneath the sand . . . like the bones of Jack the Sailor."

"Who's Jack the Sailor?" Sean asked.

"Many years ago Jack heard about the pirate

ghost," Sam said. "Jack bragged that there wasn't a pirate, alive or dead, who could get the better of him."

Sam paused, and Sean asked, "Well? What happened?"

Sam looked sorrowful. "Jack was never seen again. Except for his bones, of course, which was all that was left of him."

"Don't think about Sam's dumb ghost stories," Brian said to Sean. "Think about how we have to find Lester before we run out of time."

Sean glanced at the clock on the stove, and a chill ran up his backbone. "It's almost eight-forty-five," he exclaimed.

"What's all this about Lester?" Sam asked.

Brian took a good look at Sam. "It's … uh … confidential," he said. "But maybe you can help us. Lester disappeared during the night, and we think he may have gone to the pirate caves."

Sam's eyes shone. "If you want me to come with you, I will," he said. "Have you got another flashlight?"

Brian fished out another and gave it to Sam. "I'm glad you're here," he said.

"Oops, that reminds me," Sam said. "I came to tell you that Debbie Jean is behind a tree across the street, watching your house."

"She thinks she's following us," Sean said. "But we're going to cut out the back way and lose her."

Silently, Brian and Sean walked their bikes through a gap in the hedge. When they reached the street behind their house, Sam met them on his bike, and they took off.

Fifteen minutes later they reached the lower road that led under the cliffs along the shoreline around Hernando Cove. Brian braked to a stop. Sean and Sam pulled up behind him.

From where they stood they could look down the pile of boulders into the small cove. Dull, gray ocean water reflected the overcast sky. The tide was out, leaving a trail of gleaming brown seaweed. The sandy beach was littered with driftwood, and a battered old shack rested in the shadow near the edge of the tumbled pile of boulders. Damp fingers of mist trailed across the shack and the lower rocks. There were no signs of Lester or his bike.

"Maybe we guessed wrong," Sean said. "We can go home now."

Brian shook his head. "We need a closer look. Bring your bikes. We'll park them just a short way down the trail, behind the rocks."

As they found a hidden place in which to put their bikes, Sean said, "I don't see Lester's bike anywhere."

Brian bent over, studying the narrow trail that ran down to the cove. "He may not have come this way. I don't see footprints or marks from bike tires." Brian paused. "The road that turns into the cove is about a quarter mile farther on."

"Do you think Lester would have used the road instead of this trail?"

"In the middle of the night? Probably. Let's go down and find out."

They quickly worked their way down the narrow and crooked trail that ran between the boulders.

As they neared the bottom of the trail, Sean asked, "What if we don't find any bike tire tracks or footprints?"

Sam jumped from a low boulder to the sand and pointed toward the shack. "There are plenty of footprints," he said. "Look."

"Those are too big to be Lester's," Brian

pointed out.

They all gave a start as a voice suddenly boomed, "Go away! You kids don't belong here!"

An elderly man wearing stained khaki trousers and a tattered sweatshirt stood in the doorway of the shack. Ragged wisps of white hair poked out from under his faded baseball cap.

"We're looking for someone," Brian called to the man. He glanced past the shack to the rocks, where the hammering of ocean waves, over countless years, had worn deep caves into the rock cliff. The water level was lower now, and the cliffs were dry. Through the still-clinging morning mists, Brian could barely make out a narrow, dark entrance to the caves.

"Whoever you're lookin' for, he ain't here!" the man shouted. "No one comes around these parts. The caves are haunted. You know that, don't you?"

Brian trudged through the soft sand toward the man. As Sean and Sam followed, the man edged back into his doorway.

"I told you to go away," he said. "If you're lookin' for pirate treasure, you're in the wrong place. There's no treasure buried here. Plenty of hunters came searchin' in years gone by, but none of 'em found so much as a penny. There's nothin' good in Hernando Cove but the fishin', and I don't welcome your company."

"We don't want treasure, and we're not interested in fishing," Brian told him. "We're looking for a missing seven-year-old boy."

"No boys around here, either." The fisherman grinned, exposing yellowed teeth, some of them missing. "If any boys had enough nerve to come near the caves, the pirate ghost would get 'em, and they'd never be seen again."

His grin grew wider. "The pirate ghost carries a sword. A *bloody* sword, if you get what I mean."

Sean, his heart thumping, took a couple of steps back. "Okay. We're going," he said.

The fisherman left his shack. With his mouth still twisted in an awful, smiling grimace, he strode toward Sean and Brian.

"That goes for *all* of us," Sam said. "We're out of here!"

Sean turned and broke into a run, struggling through the soft sand until he reached the path through the boulders. As fast as he could, he scrambled upward.

Finally, he paused and dropped to a flat place in the trail. He breathed hard, trying to catch his breath.

Sam tripped and fell next to Sean. Sean was

surprised to see that Sam looked frightened. "That guy is weird," Sam said. "While he was yelling at us, all I could think about was poor old Jack the Sailor."

"Poor old Jack the Sailor has got to be somebody you made up," Brian said. He climbed up beside Sean and sat down.

"Maybe. Maybe not," Sam said. "The story seemed very real when we were down there."

Sean had to laugh. "That's funny! You scared yourself!"

"Running away was a good move, Sean," Brian whispered.

"It wasn't a move. It was for real," Sean said.

"Whatever. The fisherman will think we've given up."

"We have, haven't we?" Sean asked.

"No, we haven't," Brian said. "We haven't checked out the caves yet."

"But that guy said—"

"He said there weren't any boys around. That means he didn't see any. But if Lester came here, it was in the middle of the night and the fisherman was probably asleep."

Sean gulped. "Then the pirate ghost got him—"

"No, he didn't."

"—with his bloody sword."

"Come off it, Sean," Brian said. "Don't pay any attention to the stories Sam tells you. He just likes to scare you."

"Sam's scared, too," Sean answered.

Sam looked embarrassed. "I *was* scared for maybe a minute or two, but don't tell my little brother," he said. He looked at Sean. "The Jack-the-Sailor story wasn't exactly true, but the pirate ghost sure is."

Brian raised up, peering over the rocks,

then sat down and whispered to Sean, "The fisherman's still out there. You and Sam hide in the rocks. I'm going to ride around to the road that enters the cove and see if I can find Lester's bike, or any sign he might be here. If I do . . . Well, we'll climb down again, sneak around the shack, and enter the cave."

"With the ghost?" Sean asked.

Brian looked at his watch. "Forget the ghost. It's after ten o'clock."

Bent over, so the fisherman wouldn't see him, Brian started up the trail. Sam scrambled up next.

Sean made his own way upward, leaving the trail. But as he climbed around one of the boulders he stepped on a soft lump that suddenly moved out from under his foot. A low growl sounded in his ears, and something clamped tightly around his ankle.

5

WATCH IT," Debbie Jean grumbled. "You stepped on my foot."

Sean dropped down beside her. "What are you doing here?" he demanded.

"I'm following you," she said. "I'm the one who told you about the missing bike and the way Lester acted about his medicine. If Lester's here, then I'm going to get credit for finding him, too."

Sam slid down beside them. "Keep the noise down," he said. "We don't want the guy who lives in the shack to know we're still here."

"Why?" Debbie Jean asked.

"Because we're going to try to get into the caves and look for Lester," Sam answered. "We think that's where he's gone."

"Lester has a lot of posters and books about caves in his room," Sean added. "We're hoping they're a clue."

Debbie Jean nodded in agreement. "Lester talks about caves all the time," she told them. "I've heard him say a lot of times that someday he was going to explore the pirate caves and find the treasure."

"You didn't tell us that," Sean complained.

"You didn't ask me," Debbie Jean said.

"Did Lester know about the pirate ghost?" Sean asked.

"Sure," Debbie Jean said. "But Lester wasn't worried about ghosts." She looked at Sean. "I guess the ghost doesn't bother you, either. Huh?"

Sean pictured a pirate waving a bloody sword at him. He shrugged and said, "Not much."

Brian slid down into the hollow next to Sean. He didn't seem surprised to see Debbie Jean. "I saw your bike by the road to the cove," he said. "And I saw a green mountain bike hidden nearby it."

"Green? That's Lester's bike," Debbie Jean said.

"You were right, Bri. Lester came to the caves by way of the road." Sean frowned as he thought. "But if he's in the caves, wouldn't he have heard the fisherman talking with us? Why didn't he come out?"

"He wouldn't come out if he's hiding," Debbie Jean said.

"Or . . ." Brian stopped. "Never mind," he said. "We'll have to go in the caves and find him."

"How are we going to do that, with the fisherman there to stop us?" Sam asked.

"We'll just have to wait until he's sure we've left." Twice Brian rose to look over the rocks, but both times the fisherman was still in sight.

"He's mending a large net," Brian said. He looked at his watch again. "That could take forever."

"Maybe one of us could talk to him, and the others could sneak into the cave," Debbie Jean suggested.

"It wouldn't work," Brian said. "He'd figure out what we were up to."

For a few minutes they sat so quietly they could hear the steady splat and fizzle of small waves hitting the shore before being sucked back into the sea. Finally, Brian looked at his watch and sighed. "It's nearly noon. Time's going by awfully fast."

"See if the fisherman's still there," Sam whispered. "Maybe he'll go inside his shack and eat lunch."

Brian rose slowly, bracing himself against a large boulder. This time he motioned to the others. "He's nowhere in sight," he said. "Come on. And be quiet! We'll head for the entrance to the caves."

They climbed down the trail and walked silently through the sand, staying close to the bottom of the cliff. As they passed the shack, they bent low, hoping that the fisherman wouldn't look out his window and see them.

Slowly, step-by-step, they approached the entrance to the caves. The gash in the dark, volcanic rock seemed much larger than it had at a distance. It looked like a giant fish's open mouth, ready to swallow whoever came near.

Mists swirled around the opening, and Sean

wished the mists could turn into fog, hiding them from view. What if the fisherman saw them? What if he chased them? Sean glanced over his shoulder, toward the shack they had passed, but there was no sign of the fisherman.

Brian held up his hand for the others to stop. "It's just a couple of feet up to the entrance," he whispered. "We can get into the caves without any problems. Just be careful where you step. Caves are full of holes . . . and sometimes rats. Shine your flashlight wherever you step. Debbie Jean, since you don't have a flashlight, stick close to Sean."

"Yuck," Sean mumbled.

Debbie Jean shivered. "There are rats in the caves?" she asked. "You didn't say anything about rats."

Brian ignored her question. "If you're ready," he said, "let's go."

Before they could move, a deep, horrible yell shattered the air.

Brian, Sean, Sam, and Debbie Jean froze. They stared in horror at the entrance to the caves. Through the mists stepped a pirate, dressed like a shabby Captain Hook. A dirty bandanna was wrapped around his head, and an eye patch covered one eye.

The pirate yelled again and waved his sword, which dripped with bright red blood. He jumped from the caves' entrance to the sand and faced them.

"You're my prisoners!" he cackled. "You'll never get out of here alive!"

6

DEBBIE JEAN SCREAMED and broke into a run, heading for the road that led down to the cove.

Sean ran, too, but in the opposite direction, heading for the path up the cliff. All he wanted was his bike—the fastest way to get home!

It wasn't until Sean had reached his bike that Brian and Sam were able to catch up with him.

"Sean, stop! Where are you going?" Brian asked.

"Home!" Sean said.

Brian grabbed Sean's shoulders. "Leave the bike there."

"And let the ghost get us?"

"The ghost isn't going to get us ... or anybody else."

"Don't make promises you can't keep." Sam's voice shook.

Above them they heard the swish of bike tires and saw Debbie Jean speeding past.

Sean made another try at pulling out of Brian's grip. "Let me go!" he said. "We've got to get out of here."

"No. We're going back," Brian said.

"We can't. You saw the ghost!"

"I think I like Sean's idea best," Sam said.

Brian shook his head. "I *did* take a good look at the ghost. That's why we're going back."

Sean stopped tugging and turned to look at Brian. "What's that supposed to mean?"

"It means that a private investigator has to pay attention to details. Didn't you notice anything unusual about the pirate?"

Sean shivered as he remembered the pirate. "The dirty clothes he was wearing? The blood dripping from his sword?"

"His *teeth*," Brian said. "Some of them were missing . . . just like the fisherman's teeth. In fact, the very same teeth."

"Wait a minute," Sean said. "Are you telling us that the fisherman dressed up like a pirate?"

"Yes."

"Why would he want to scare people and make them run away?"

"I don't know," Brian answered. "Maybe he's still searching for pirate treasure he wants to keep for himself."

Sam interrupted. "He told us there wasn't any treasure. He said people had looked for years and hadn't found any."

Brian shrugged. "Maybe he wasn't telling the truth. Or maybe he just wants to live alone in peace and quiet without a lot of people around. Whatever his reason, I'm sure of one thing: The pirate we saw is not a ghost."

Sean thought a moment. "He was pretty scary. He would have scared Lester away, too."

"Not if the fisherman had been asleep. Remember what I told you. If Lester came here to the caves, it was during the night."

Sean shuddered. "That wasn't Lester's blood on the sword, was it?"

"It wasn't anybody's blood," Brian said. "If we'd been closer we probably would have smelled ketchup."

Sean wouldn't give up. "But the pirate made a lot of noise. How come Lester didn't hear him?"

"The pirate was standing at the entrance of the caves," Brian said. "Lester would have had to run right into him."

"He could have yelled for help."

"The pirate or Lester?" Sam said.

"Look, Sean's right. We haven't heard a sound from Lester," Brian said. "That worries me."

Sean leaned against one of the boulders. "How are we going to go back to the caves without running into the pirate again?"

"Easy," Brian answered. "The pirate thinks he's scared us and we've run home. We'll leave our bikes here and climb down the trail again."

"He won't see us?"

"Not if we're careful. I saw what looks like another trail branching off the one that drops down to the beach. I don't know how far it goes, but we can try it. That way we'll be hidden by the rocks as we go behind the shack. Hopefully, we can stay hidden all the way to the caves' entrance."

Brian looked at Sean and Sam. "Are you coming with me to look for Lester?"

Sean gulped, then answered, "We have to find him. I'll come."

Sam didn't seem very happy about the idea, but he said, "We haven't got a choice. I'll come, too."

It was hard going. The trail grew narrow, then disappeared entirely. Brian climbed the nearest boulder to look around, then jumped down to where Sean was standing.

"No problem," he said. "The shack's right below us. I just saw the fisherman go inside. He was whistling and looked pleased with himself. He's sure now that he scared us away."

Sean looked at the boulders ahead. "Where do we go now?"

"We'll climb over the rocks. Just a little way farther they'll be like stepping-stones down to the mouth of the caves."

Sean shuddered as he thought about the gaping hole in the rocks and the gaping mouth of the pirate-fisherman. "Yuck! Don't say *mouth*," he said. "It makes me think of being swallowed."

Brian led the way. Carefully, he, Sean, and Sam inched their way up and over the pile of boulders.

Just as Brian had said, going down was a lot easier. Soon they reached the ledge of dark rock that stretched over the sand. A few feet away loomed the entrance to the caves.

Brian put a finger to his lips and pointed to a pocket of sand that had drifted into the entrance. At one side, where it mounded against the rock wall, were small shoe prints.

"Lester's in here somewhere," he whispered.

Sean, Brian, and Sam quickly slipped inside the cave. Sean cautiously poked his head out to see if there was any sign of the fisherman. "He didn't see us, Bri," he said and leaned against the wall with a sigh of relief.

But the wall curved inward, and Sean went with it, staggering to stay on his feet. In this hidden spot something rough and scratchy swung over his head, brushing his cheek. "Yikes!" Sean cried. He jumped back, crashing into Brian, who had followed him.

"Be quiet," Brian said.

"But something . . ." He looked up to see a headless pirate swinging slowly against the wall. "Yikes!" he shouted again.

"It's only the pirate costume," Brian said. "It's hanging on a piece of rock that's jutting out."

"I thought it was the ghost."

"Stop scaring yourself. I told you, there aren't any ghosts in here."

Sean's eyes grew accustomed to the dim light that filtered into the black stone walls of this pocket in the cave. He could clearly see the costume. "I'm glad nothing was inside it," he said. "No pirates. No ghosts."

A battered old sword lay on the ground. It had been wiped clean, but the rag next to it was covered with ketchup.

Sean and Brian stepped back into the main room of the cave. Sam turned on his flashlight and aimed the beam for the back wall. "It narrows there," he said, "but I can see some kind of opening—maybe into another cavern."

Brian studied the area. "The opening seems large enough to walk through," he said.

"How far back does this cave go?" Sean asked.

"I don't know," Brian answered. "It could be quite a long way. We'll find out."

Sean turned on his flashlight. He swung the beam of light on the ragged pirate costume. "Good-bye, old pirate," he said, and laughed. "No ghosts allowed in here."

But in the stillness, from the depths of the cave, came a long, soft, mournful wail.

7

SEAN GASPED AND yelled, "I'm outta here!"

Brian grabbed Sean's shoulder. "Don't panic," he told him.

"You said there were no ghosts in here."

"Right," Sam said. "I heard you say it."

"That wasn't a ghost we heard. It was probably Lester."

Sean stopped struggling and looked at Brian. "Lester made that awful, scary sound?"

"That's what we have to find out. Lester may be scared or even hurt."

"Or just trying to scare us," Sean said.

Sam glanced into the blackness that lay behind the narrow turn in the cave. "Should we go for help?"

"Not yet. First, let's see what's going on."

Brian, Sean, and Sam squeezed through the narrow passage and around the corner, their flashlights lighting the way. They found themselves in a large cavern with rough walls and an uneven floor.

Brian put out a hand to hold Sean back. "Look out," he said. "There may be holes in the cave floor or it may be thin in places. We don't want you to fall through."

"How come all of a sudden you know so much about caves?" Sean asked.

"We had Mr. Caney for science last year," Sam said.

"Yeah. He's a spelunker," Brian said.

"Spelunkers explore caves. Mr. Caney liked to talk about his adventures, but he also warned us about the dangers."

Sean turned his flashlight on the rough walls, discovering holes where the rock had been worn away by the waves that had once pounded against it. On the other side of the cave were deeper holes that looked like openings into other caverns. "There must be other rooms in this cave," Sean said. "If Lester *did* come in here, which way would he have gone?"

"I'll see if he answers us," Brian said. He called loudly, "Lester! Where are you?"

Again, a mournful wail rose around them. Sean grabbed Brian's arm. "That noise came out of the ground," he whispered.

Brian pulled away from Sean and took a cautious step forward. "Lester!" he yelled. "Answer us. We have to know where you are."

The wail turned into a whimper, and a small voice cried, "I'm down here."

Brian dropped to his knees. "Stay where you are," he told Sam and Sean. The cave floor was icy cold, and the dampness seeped into Brian's jeans. Carefully, testing the floor as he crawled, he made his way toward a dark patch that lay ahead.

"Talk to us, Lester," he said. "Keep talking. Let us know where you are."

Lester stopped crying. He coughed, then asked, "Who are you?"

"I'm Brian Quinn. My brother Sean is with me, and Sam Miyako is here, too."

"I want my mother," Lester demanded. "And my father. Why aren't they here?"

"Because they don't know where you are," Brian said. As he inched forward, he saw that the dark patch was a jagged hole in the cave floor.

"If they don't know, how come *you* know?" Lester demanded.

"We're private investigators," Brian said. "We followed the clues."

Sean called to Lester, "Yeah, and they believed your ransom note. We didn't."

"It was a good ransom note!" Lester shouted angrily. He went into a coughing fit and Brian turned to shake his head at Sean.

"Don't make him mad," Brian whispered to Sean. "We've got to get him out of here."

Brian slid on his stomach to the edge of the hole and aimed his flashlight beam downward. He gasped as he saw that the hole was so deep that the light couldn't break through the blackness.

Just below Brian, about ten feet down, was a narrow ledge. On this ledge, at the edge of the dark pit, lay Lester Hopper.

"I hurt my ankle!" Lester moaned. "I can't stand up." He wiggled impatiently. "Get me out of here! What's taking you so long?"

Brian held his breath as a loose piece of rock crumbled from the ledge and bounced into the blackness.

"Lester, don't move," Brian said firmly. "You've got to stay quiet. You're lying on a ledge that couldn't be more that four feet wide."

"Stop telling me what to do!" Lester squirmed again. "Just get me out of here." He scowled. "And don't think you're going to make me take that awful medicine, because I won't."

"We don't even have your dumb old medicine," Sean called.

Brian spoke firmly to Lester. "You don't want to fall over the side like those rocks did, so do what I said—don't move. We're going to have to get help to get you out of there."

"I'll ask the fisherman to call 911," Sam said.

Brian twisted toward Sam. "I don't think the fisherman has a phone. You'll have to ride back to town. Get the police, the firemen, the paramedics. And call my dad."

"I'm on my way," Sam said. He backed up and left the cave.

"Sean," Brian said, "I'll stay with Lester. You get the fisherman. Bring him in here."

"He tried to scare us away," Sean said. "What makes you think he'll help us."

"He'll help. Tell him to bring his lantern and a lot of strong rope. And be careful! Watch for holes!"

Sean shook so hard, the beam from his flashlight wobbled ahead of him, making a wiggly light show on the walls and floor of the cave.

Daylight streamed through the opening to the world outside, and Sean rushed toward it. He burst through, tripping on the rock ledge and sprawling onto the sand below.

He picked himself up, turned off his flashlight, and stuck it in his belt. As fast as possible, Sean struggled through the deep sand until he came to the fisherman's shack. Although Sean was afraid of meeting the fisherman face-to-face, he pounded on the door of the shack.

"Help!" he yelled. "You've got to help us!"

Sean took a step backward and tensed, waiting for the fisherman to come storming out. But nothing happened.

Puzzled, Sean hammered on the door again.

When it didn't open, Sean turned the handle. The door easily slid open. Stacks of old newspapers lined one wall, and dirty dishes were piled in a pan next to a small butane gas stove. But there was no sign of the fisherman. The shack was empty.

"We need you! Where are you?" Sean shouted. He knew it would take at least a half hour for other help to arrive. They couldn't leave Lester on that narrow ledge all that time.

Sean ran down the beach and scanned the bay. In the distance, too far away to hear Sean's yells, the fisherman sat in a tiny rowboat.

"Come back!" Sean screamed to him. But the fisherman didn't hear. He didn't even glance in Sean's direction.

Sean rubbed at a tear that rolled down his cheek. He had to do something to bring the fisherman back. But what? What was he going to do?

8

FIRE! SEAN THOUGHT. The fisherman might not be able to hear him, but he could see him—especially if Sean attracted his attention with a fiery torch.

Sean dashed back to the shack and burst through the door. He grabbed some newspapers and rolled them together into a tight cone about six feet long. He dipped the end in a can that smelled like bacon grease. Then Sean snatched a matchbook that lay near the stove. He ran back outside to the water's edge.

His fingers trembled, but he managed to

light the third match he tried. He held it to the dripping top of the newspaper cone, shielding it from the breeze until the fire caught and was blazing nicely.

Sean waved the torch in the air and shouted again at the fisherman.

Suddenly the man looked in Sean's direction and jumped with alarm. He put down his pole and began to row quickly toward the shore.

Sean shoved what was left of the burning newspaper cone into the water's edge, and the fire went out with a sizzle.

It seemed like forever to Sean until the rowboat pulled up on the sand and the angry fisherman leaped out.

"What do you think you're doing?" he yelled at Sean.

Sean jumped back out of reach. "We need your help!" he said. "There's a little boy trapped in a hole in the caves."

The fisherman's anger turned to fear. "I told you kids not to go in there!" he cried out.

"We had to!" Sean said, and he quickly told the fisherman about Lester running away in the middle of the night.

The fisherman groaned. "I try everything I can to keep the kids away from those caves. I even dress like the ghost," he said. "Nobody realizes how dangerous those caves can be."

"Maybe Lester doesn't know about your ghost," Sean said. "Or maybe he doesn't care. He's kind of ... well ... used to getting his own way."

"Where is he?" the fisherman asked.

"In the second cavern," Sean told him. "Lester fell through a hole in the floor. He's lying on a ledge. He said he hurt his ankle. My brother Brian is with him. Our friend rode his bike back to town to get help." Sean shivered. "Bri's afraid that Lester might fall off the ledge before the rescue teams get here, so he told me to ask you to bring your lantern and lots of strong rope."

The fisherman strode so quickly toward his shack that Sean had to run to keep up. "Come with me," the fisherman said. "You can help me carry the things we'll need."

He lit two lanterns, handing both to Sean, then picked up something that looked like a tangle of leather straps.

"What's that?" Sean asked.

"An old harness," the fisherman answered. "The kind that sailors once wore in heavy seas to make sure they wouldn't fall overboard."

He looped coils of the rope over his shoulder, staggering under the weight, and reached for something made of metal. "Lead the way," he said to Sean. "Show me where to find this boy."

Once inside the cave, Sean and the fisherman moved cautiously. Sean could hear the man's heavy breathing and see the drops of sweat running down his face. The fisherman was scared, and that frightened Sean even more. Grown-ups were supposed to stay calm and say things like "Everything's going to be okay, I'll take care of it," so kids could relax.

As they entered the second cavern, Sean could hear Brian talking to Lester. The lantern light flashed on the damp walls, lighting the cavern. Brian looked up, and Sean could see the fear in his eyes, too.

"Thanks for coming," he said to the fisherman. "Lester's down here."

The fisherman squirmed slowly and carefully to the edge of the hole and looked down. "Can you stand up, son?" he asked. "If I send down a harness to you, can you put it on and fasten the buckles?"

"No!" Lester cried. "My ankle hurts. I want my mother and father! Where are they?" Angrily, he hit the cave wall with his fist. A handful of small rocks broke off and bounced from the ledge.

"Cut that out," Brian said sharply. "Any more temper tantrums and you could find yourself falling off the ledge into that deep pit."

"Stop it! You're trying to scare me!" Lester yelled.

Brian spoke quietly to the fisherman. "Lester might have broken his ankle when he fell down there. If he tries to stand up, or even sit up, he could pitch right off that ledge." He shuddered. "He might do that anyway."

"Then somebody's got to go down there and put the harness on him," the fisherman said.

"I will," Brian offered.

"No, you won't," the man told him. "It'll be me alone trying to lower you and bring you up, and I don't know if I can manage it. You'd be too heavy."

Brian and the fisherman turned at the same time to look at Sean.

"Oh, no you don't!" Brian said. "I can't let Sean go down there. It's too dangerous."

"I'll tie him up good and tight," the fisherman said. "I brought a pulley and plenty of rope. I'll find something sturdy somewhere on the cave walls that we can loop the ropes through. With the two of us on the ropes—one for your brother and one for the boy on the ledge—we can haul them up, one at a time."

Sean took a deep breath, but his voice wobbled. "I can do it," he told Brian.

"No," Brian said.

"What are you waiting for? Get me out of here!" Lester yelled. He began to sob.

The fisherman backed away from the hole on his hands and knees. When his shoes bumped the side of the cave he stumbled to his feet. For a moment he took some long breaths to steady himself. Then he called to Sean, "Bring one of those lanterns over here."

Peering closely at the rough walls, the fisherman ran his fingers over them. In a few minutes he straightened and tugged hard at a section where the rock had worn through, leaving a four-inch pillar of rock that reached from the bottom to the top of the cave.

"This is just what we need," he said. "I can pull the ropes through the opening, and they'll hold."

Lester cried out again. "Don't leave me

down here!"

Sean looked at the dark hole in the cave floor. Then he looked at Brian. "Let me go down and get Lester, Bri," he said.

They heard a thump and a crash. Hands shaking, Brian aimed the flashlight down at Lester. A piece of the ledge, just beyond Lester's feet, had broken off.

"What happened?" Brian asked.

"I don't know," Lester mumbled. "I just kicked a little bit."

"I told you to lie still," Brian said.

Lester scowled. "It's your fault. You didn't come down here to get me."

"We're coming now," Brian said. He crawled back to join the fisherman. "Are you sure Sean won't be in danger?"

"Not as long as we're hanging on to him," the man answered. He pulled tight the knots that fastened the second rope to the leather harness.

"How do I put the harness on Lester?" Sean asked.

The fisherman hurried to explain. Then he fastened one end of the rope to the wall and the pulley. With the other end he made a harness that fit over Sean's shoulders, around his chest and back, and under his legs.

As he pulled the knots tight, he said, "When you get to the ledge, fasten the leather harness on the boy. Make sure all the straps are pulled tight and buckled. We'll haul him up first, then bring you after him. Okay?"

"Okay," Sean said, but the words came out in a squeak. He cleared his throat and tried again. "Okay," he repeated.

With the harness for Lester over his right arm and shoulder, Sean crawled to the edge of the hole and looked down. The lantern light barely reached the ledge.

"Ease yourself over," the fisherman said. "We've got a good grip on you. We'll lower you slowly. When you reach the ledge, give us a holler."

Sean, tightly clinging to the rope, felt himself dropping inch by inch. Finally his toes touched something, and he scrambled to get a foothold.

He had reached the ledge and was standing about a foot away from Lester's head.

"I'm down!" Sean yelled to the fisherman.

But suddenly the chunk of rock on which Sean was standing gave way, and he swung out, over the dark pit.

9

SEAN'S YELL ECHOED in the cave, hurting his ears. Panting, he tried to reach the ledge again, and once more felt something solid under his feet. "I'm okay!" he cried, but he didn't feel okay. He felt dizzy and sick and wished he were home in bed.

"What are you doing?" Lester asked him.

"I'm helping you," Sean said. He tested the ledge with his weight and found that this time it held.

"Give me more rope," he shouted, and as the rope eased, he was able to kneel next to Lester.

"Put this on," he said. "We'll put your feet through first."

"Don't touch my ankle," Lester said.

"I've got to," Sean said. "It may hurt a little bit, but this is the only way we can get you out of this hole."

Lester whimpered, but he let Sean pull the harness around his legs and up to his hips.

"Now, put one arm in," Sean directed. As Lester did what Sean said, Sean eased Lester's other arm into the harness. Finally, he buckled the leather straps around Lester's hips and chest, making sure they were tight.

"They're going to pull you up now," Sean said.

"Will I swing in the air, like you did?"

"Sure," Sean told him.

Lester's lip curled out. "I don't want to."

"You have to," Sean said. He called out,

"Lester's ready to come up!"

The rope attached to Lester's harness began to tighten. It pulled him to a sitting position.

"I said I didn't want to!" Lester screamed.

"Don't be afraid," Sean said. "You'll be out of here in a few minutes."

Inch by inch, Lester was pulled upright and off his feet. Screaming all the way, he was dragged up to the cave floor. Sean saw the fisherman grab Lester by the shoulders and yank him up out of sight.

"Now me," Sean said to himself. He gulped as he glanced at the black pit, less than a foot away from his toes. He closed his eyes and breathed evenly, trying to stay calm, but it seemed like hours before he heard Brian call, "Sean, are you ready?"

"Ready!" Sean yelled.

The rope tightened as Sean was jerked

upward.

Sean clung to the rope and stared upward at the dim light. Bri was up there. So was the fisherman. They'd get him out of this awful place.

With strong arms holding him, Sean scrambled onto the cave floor and quickly crawled away from the hole. For a few minutes he lay on his stomach, head pillowed on his arms, and tried to breathe normally.

But Brian grabbed him. "Sean!" Brian shouted. "That was cool! That was cooler that cool! You were terrific!"

His fingers fumbled with the knots in the rope around Sean, untying them.

"You did a fine job," the fisherman said.

He scooped up Lester, who grumbled at Sean, "My ankle hurts. You bumped it."

Brian and Sean collected the rope and the

lanterns and followed the pirate out of the cave. As they reached the entrance they could hear sirens.

Brian looked at his watch. "It's almost two-thirty. Lester will get back in time to take his medicine."

"I'm not going to take my medicine! Ever!" Lester shouted. "That's why I ran away."

The fisherman looked into Lester's face, almost nose-to-nose. "You'll take your medicine, or the pirate ghost who haunts these caves will make you walk the plank."

"I didn't see any pirate ghost," Lester said.

"You didn't? He was there. He saw *you*."

Lester's lower lip stuck out. "How's he going to make me take my medicine if I don't want to?"

"If I were you, I wouldn't try to find out." The fisherman's mouth twisted into a gap-toothed grin, and he chuckled a horrible laugh, low in his throat.

"I want my mother!" Lester shrieked.

A parade of cars, led by the sheriff's cruiser and an ambulance, turned into the cove.

Lester's parents ran toward him. His mother waved the medicine bottle and a spoon. Lester glanced up at the fisherman, who growled. When his mother reached him and held out a spoonful of the medicine, Lester gulped and swallowed it without a complaint.

As the paramedics tended to Lester's injured ankle, the fisherman sighed. "People will come around the caves again, once you tell them I dressed up like a pirate ghost."

"Sean and I aren't going to tell them," Brian said. "We all saw the ghost. Remember his sword dripping with blood?"

"What about Sam?" Sean said. "He knows

who the ghost is, too."

"I'll tell Sam to keep it quiet as soon as I see him," Brian said. "Sam's going to have great fun scaring his little brother and everybody else who'll listen when he tells them he personally met the pirate ghost."

Mr. Quinn drove up, and Sam and Debbie Jean jumped from his car.

"You found Lester!" Debbie Jean shouted. "And all because of me!"

There were introductions to be made and questions to be answered. True to his promise, Brian pulled Sam aside and told him to keep quiet about the ghost's identity. Sam quickly agreed.

Finally, to Sean and Brian's relief, they piled into Mr. Quinn's car with Debbie Jean and Sam.

Brian quickly told their dad why they'd

come looking for Lester at the caves.

"I saw your note," he said. "That was good thinking on your part. If Mr. and Mrs. Hopper had been honest with me about what really happened, we might have found Lester much sooner."

He glanced at Brian and Sean and added, "Now, tell me where you found Lester and what happened."

"Uh . . . in the second cavern, Dad. Lester was hiding in the caves," Brian said.

"You went into those caves?"

Sean interrupted. "Start the car, Dad. Wait till we get home. Then we'll tell you all about it."

"You know the caves are dangerous," Mr. Quinn said. "I'm not happy with the idea that you were inside them."

Debbie Jean stared at Sean, open-mouthed.

"You really, truly went into the caves, even after that awful pirate ghost warned us away?"

"Debbie Jean keeps insisting that you saw a pirate ghost," Mr. Quinn said.

He smiled, and Sean was thankful that he and Brian weren't in really big trouble.

"Take Debbie Jean's word for it, Dad," Brian said. He grinned at Sam and Sean.

As Debbie Jean began to describe the ghost again, Brian turned to wave good-bye to the fisherman, who stood at the door to his shack, watching them. Brian nudged Sean, who glanced back, too, as the fisherman raised a hand and waved.

But from the shadows near the entrance to the caves, a ghostly pirate stepped out. He held his sword high in a salute.

"Bri!" Sean whispered. "The fisherman didn't say he *was* the ghost. He said he dressed like the ghost! That means . . ."

"Everybody be quiet," Debbie Jean ordered. "I'm the one telling about the ghost. It's my turn."

For a moment Brian looked wide-eyed at Sean. Then he slid back in the seat and slowly began to smile. "Face it, Sean," he said. "This may be the first mystery in which the Casebusters didn't come up with all the answers."

JOAN LOWERY NIXON is a renowned writer of children's mysteries. She is the author of more than eighty books and the only four-time recipient of the prestigious Edgar Allan Poe Award for the best juvenile mystery of the year.

❪

"I was asked by Disney Adventures *magazine if I could write a short mystery. I decided to write about two young boys who help their father, a private investigator, solve crimes. These boys, Brian and Sean, are actually based on my grandchildren, who are the same ages as the characters. My first Casebusters story was a piece about a ghost that haunts an inn. This derives from a legendary Louisiana inn I visited which was allegedly haunted. Later, I learned the owner had made up the entire tale, and I used that angle in the story."*

Beware the Pirate Ghost

Here's a secret code from the Casebusters! You can use it to write messages to your friends and to decode the Casebusters' Crimesolving Tip below.

Secret Code

Replace each letter in your message with the fifth letter after it in the alphabet.

A = F	J = O	S = X
B = G	K = P	T = Y
C = H	L = Q	U = Z
D = I	M = R	V = A
E = J	N = S	W = B
F = K	O = T	X = C
G = L	P = U	Y = D
H = M	Q = V	Z = E
I = N	R = W	

Secret Message

Hfxjgzxyjwx Hwnrjxtqansl Ynk #7
Nk dtz ymnsp dtz'wj gjnsl ktqqtbji, yzws f kjb
htwsjwx fsi hmjhp yt xjj bmjymjw ymj ujwxts yzwsx,
ytt. Ymj ujwxts yfnqnsl dtz rfd uzy ts f inxlznxj, xt
hmjhp ktw ymnslx ymfy fwj inkknhzqy yt hmfslj, qnpj
xmtjx, xpns ytsj, fsi flj.